*This book is dedicated to Hameed Ali, founder of the
Ridhwan Foundation and the Diamond Heart and Training Institute,
as he has led the way for so many to unveil their essential value.*

Peggy O'Neill

*To my husband Craig, who has helped me find my
courage, confidence and compassion. And to my children,
Donia and Earl, may you find courage, confidence
and compassion in your own lives.*

Denise Freeman

Little Squarehead

Story by Peggy O'Neill
Illustrations by Denise Freeman

ILLUMINATION ARTS PUBLISHING, INC.

Once upon a time there was a little girl named Rosa who lived in a small town nestled against a lush emerald forest. She loved playing in the woods with her animal friends. They didn't mind that she looked different from the other children – her head was shaped like a square.

Rosa didn't like walking through town, because so many people would stop and stare at her. Even though she pretended not to notice, this always hurt her feelings.

One day when Rosa was on her way home from school, some children pointed at her and started chanting, "There goes Rosa Redhead. She's a Little Squarehead."

Rosa ran away deep into the forest until she came to a glistening stream. "Why do I have to look so different?" she cried. "I'll never have any friends!"

As her tears fell, an enchanting mist arose from the water, and a sweet, musical voice called out, "Rosa dear, don't cry. All will be well."

Rosa followed the soothing voice to a crystal pool. "Look into the water," whispered the voice.

Rosa knelt on the grass and glanced at her reflection. She was amazed to see a brilliant diamond sparkling in her heart. "Oh!" she gasped, "What is that?"

"It is the reflection of your true self," said the musical voice. "Now you know who you really are."

"I already know who I am,"Rosa said. "I'm just an ugly girl with a square head!"

The pond rippled as the voice replied, "That's not true, Rosa dear. You are beautiful and precious beyond compare. I'm here to help you see yourself in this way. Return here tomorrow and you will receive a priceless gift."

"*T*hank you! Thank you!" Rosa shouted.
For the first time ever, someone had called her
beautiful. Bursting with joy, she skipped all
the way home.

After school the next day, a group of children pointed at Rosa and laughed, "Here comes Rosa Redhead. She's a Little Squarehead."

This time, instead of crying, Rosa thought of the diamond in her heart.

Holding her head high, she just smiled and walked away. Then she hurried back to the secret pool to see what her priceless gift might be.

Rosa was so excited that she waded into the water and gazed at her reflection. "It's still there!" she gasped.

"Remember," said the musical voice, "this diamond mirrors the beauty that already shines within you."

"Yes, I can feel it," said Rosa. Then she looked around to see if she could spot her gift. "Do you have something for me?" she asked.

The voice laughed. "You have already found it – the gift of **COURAGE**. This will help you to always be brave and strong. Return tomorrow and you will discover another priceless gift."

At recess the following day, Rosa saw some girls playing hopscotch. She started to walk away as usual, but then suddenly felt a glow in her heart. Turning back, she surprised herself by saying, "I'd like to draw a picture. May I borrow your chalk?"

By the time recess had ended, all the girls were drawing pictures together. "That was fun," Rosa said. "Let's play again tomorrow."

*L*ater that afternoon Rosa hurried back to the pool.
"I made some friends today!" she announced joyfully.
"It doesn't matter to them that my head is square."

Soft music filled the air. "Rosa dear," said the voice, "you
now have the gift of **CONFIDENCE**. This will help you to
follow your heart and believe in yourself. If you return
tomorrow, another priceless gift will be yours."

On her way to school the next morning, Rosa noticed something she had never seen before. "Oh my!" she exclaimed. "No matter how different people look on the outside, they all have sparkling diamond hearts on the inside."

After school, Rosa couldn't wait to visit her secret place. Kneeling beside the pool, she said, "Today I saw a diamond shining in everyone's heart. Is that my third gift?"

"Yes," whispered the musical voice. "You've discovered the gift of **COMPASSION** – the ability to feel your connection with everyone and everything. Those who have compassion treat others with kindness, love and respect.

"You now have all the gifts you need. But, if you ever feel sad and lonely again, just look inside your heart."

Even though she still looked different from other children, Rosa knew that she would never again be lonely Little Squarehead. Her newfound gifts of courage, confidence and compassion had changed her life forever. From that day on, it would be her sparkling diamond heart she would share with the world.

ILLUMINATION Arts

PUBLISHING COMPANY, INC.
P.O. Box 1865, Bellevue, WA 98009
Tel: 425-644-7185 ❀ 888-210-8216 (orders only) ❀ Fax: 425-644-9274
liteinfo@illumin.com ❀ www.illumin.com
Second printing 2007

❀ ❀ ❀ ❀

Library of Congress Cataloging-in-Publication Data

O'Neill, Peggy 1955-
    Little Squarehead / written by Peggy O'Neill, illustrated by Denise Freeman.
        p. cm.
    Summary: A child who is laughed at because of her square head learns to see her own inner beauty as well as that of others.
    ISBN 978-0-935699-21-0
    [1. Individuality–fiction. 2. Self-acceptance–fiction. I. Freeman, Denise, 1960-ill. II. Title.

PZ7.05564 Li 2001
[E]dc21   00-054064

Published in the United States of America
Printed in Singapore by Tien Wah Press
Book Designer: Murrah & Company, Kirkland, WA
Art Production: Cheryl Kerry of Tahoma Organic, Tacoma, WA

ILLUMINATION ARTS PUBLISHING COMPANY, INC.
is a member of Publishers in Partnership – replanting our nation's forests.

Play Hide & Seek

Now that Rosa has found her true self, she wants to tell all of her animal friends about the sparkling diamond inside each one of them. But she needs your help! Can you find all of Rosa's animal friends that are hidden throughout the book? Be careful, many of them are very good at hiding.

Title page: Cardinal, mouse, rabbit, squirrel, 2 bumblebees and 2 fish.

Pages 2-3:   Cardinal, rabbit, squirrel, wasp and 10 leaf hoppers.

Pages 4-5:   Cardinal, squirrel, 2 mice, 2 butterflies, 2 parrots, 3 cats and 16 rabbits.

Pages 6-7:   Rabbit, squirrel, wasp, little green snake, 2 cats, 2 butterflies and 3 cardinals.

Pages 8-9:   Cardinal, porcupine, deer, rabbit, squirrel, 2 mice, 2 fish and 5 lizards.

Pages 10-11:   Cardinal, mouse, rabbit, squirrel, 3 fish and 5 dragonflies.

Pages 12-13:   Cardinal, rabbit, squirrel and 2 fish.

Pages 14-15:   Cardinal, owl, deer, porcupine, raccoon, snail, squirrel, turtle, 2 mice, 3 rabbits and 5 butterflies.

Pages 16-17:   Cardinal, rabbit, squirrel and 12 caterpillars.

Pages 18-19:   Cardinal, porcupine, rabbit, squirrel, fish, 2 mice and 4 turtles.

Pages 20-21:   Cardinal, rabbit, squirrel, 2 cats, 2 mice, 6 geckos and 6 walking stick insects.

Pages 22-23:   Cardinal, rabbit, deer, raccoon, squirrel, 2 fish, 3 mice and 3 rabbits.

Pages 24-25:   Cardinal, cat, rabbit, squirrel, 2 mice and 5 bluebirds.

Pages 26-27:   Cardinal, rabbit, squirrel, 2 mice, 3 butterflies and 8 ladybugs.

Pages 28-29:   Cardinal, rabbit, squirrel, 2 mice, 2 rabbits and 12 butterflies.

Rosa's Roses

Rosa and her animal friends love to smell all of the different roses that bloom in the emerald forest. Below is a list of the roses shown in this book.

Title page:	Perfect Moment	Pages 10-11:	Rosa Eleganteria	Pages 20-21:	Rollercoaster
Pages 2-3:	Graceland	Pages 12-13:	Timeless	Pages 22-23:	Secret
Pages 4-5:	Double Delight	Pages 14-15:	Blueberry Hill	Pages 24-25:	Danae
Pages 6-7:	Cherry Brandy	Pages 16-17:	Touch of Class	Pages 26-27:	Cornelia
Pages 8-9:	Nuits de Young	Pages 18-19:	Casino	Pages 28-29:	Sterling Silver

More inspiring picture books from Illumination Arts

Just Imagine
John M. Thompson and George Schultz/Wodin, ISBN 978-0-9740190-6-2
Ready for fun and adventure? Who knows what might happen as we set our minds free and our imaginations take flight! Anything is possible when we *Just Imagine.*

Something Special
Terri Cohlene/Doug Keith, ISBN 978-0-9740190-1-7
A curious little frog finds a mysterious gift outside his home near the castle moat. It's *Something Special…*What can it be?

Am I a Color Too?
Heidi Cole/Nancy Vogl/Gerald Purnell, ISBN 978-0-9740190-5-5
A young interracial boy wonders why people are labeled by the color of their skin. Seeing that people dream, feel, sing, dance and love regardless of their color, he asks, *Am I a Color, Too?*

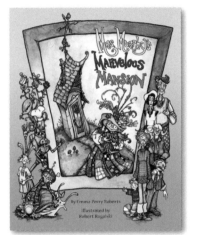

Mrs. Murphy's Marvelous Mansion
Emma Roberts/Robert Rogalski, ISBN 978-0-9740190-4-8
Mrs. Murphy's snobbish neighbors are convinced that her strange little house should be torn down – until she invites them to come for lunch. As they wander through *Mrs. Murphy's Marvelous Mansion*, the neighbors have a surprising change of heart, learning that beauty on the inside matters more than beauty on the outside.

Little Yellow Pear Tomatoes
Demian Elainé Yumei/Nicole Tamarin, ISBN 978-0-9740190-2-4
In this enchanting story, we ponder the never-ending circle of life through the eyes of a young girl, who marvels at all the energy and collaboration it takes to grow *Little Yellow Pear Tomatoes.*

We Share One World
Jane E. Hoffelt/Marty Husted, ISBN 978-0-9701907-8-9
Wherever we live – whether we work in the fields, the waterways, the mountains or the cities – all people and creatures share one world.

A Mother's Promise
Lisa Humphrey/David Danioth, ISBN 978-0-9701907-9-6
A lifetime of sharing begins with the sacred vow a woman makes to her unborn child… *A Mother's Promise.*

Your Father Forever
Travis Griffith/Raquel Abreu, ISBN 978-0-9740190-3-1
A devoted father promises to guide, protect and respect his beloved children. Transcending the boundaries of culture and time, this is the perfect expression of a parent's never-ending love.

To view our whole collection, please visit us at **www.illumin.com**.